This Little Tiger book belongs to:

_____

_____

_____

For Rosa Nella, and may she always
climb the right sort of trees ~ N L

For Hannah ~ S M

LITTLE TIGER PRESS LTD,
1 Coda Studios, 189 Munster Road, London SW6 6AW
www.littletiger.co.uk

First published in Great Britain 2007
This edition published 2018

Text copyright © Norbert Landa 2007
Illustrations copyright © Simon Mendez 2007
Norbert Landa and Simon Mendez have asserted their rights to be
identified as the author and illustrator of this work under the Copyright,
Designs and Patents Act, 1988

Little Bear
and the
Wishing Tree

Norbert Landa

Simon Mendez

LITTLE TIGER
LONDON

Bertie and Baby Bear were playing. Bertie was driving his car round the room and Baby Bear was chasing after him.

"My turn, now," said Baby Bear.

"No," said Bertie. "It's my car!"
  "Please," wailed Baby Bear.
  "Why don't you let him have a go?"
said Mummy Bear.
  "Because he always breaks my things,"
said Bertie, feeling very cross.

He ran outside
and slammed the
door behind him.

Bertie played by himself for a
while. When he peeped through
the window he saw Mummy
Bear making pancakes for tea,
and Baby Bear helping her.

He decided to climb up
his favourite tree and sit
on his favourite branch.
"I'm going to stay here
all night," he said.

Bertie's tummy rumbled. He was very hungry! He thought of Mummy Bear and Baby Bear eating pancakes and he sighed.

"Do you want something to eat?" some squirrels asked him, and brought him some berries. But they were not quite right for a little bear who was hungry.

"Thank you very much," said Bertie, and he sighed again.

And then Bertie saw a pancake hanging from a branch! "Yum, yum," he said. "I never knew this was a pancake tree!"

There were as many as he could eat and more! Bertie munched the pancakes happily.

"Want some?" he asked the squirrels. "There's plenty for everyone."

When the sun set it grew cold.
Bertie hugged his knees.

"You look chilly," some birds
said, and they gave him a couple
of feathers to cover himself. But
they were not quite right for a
little bear who was cold.

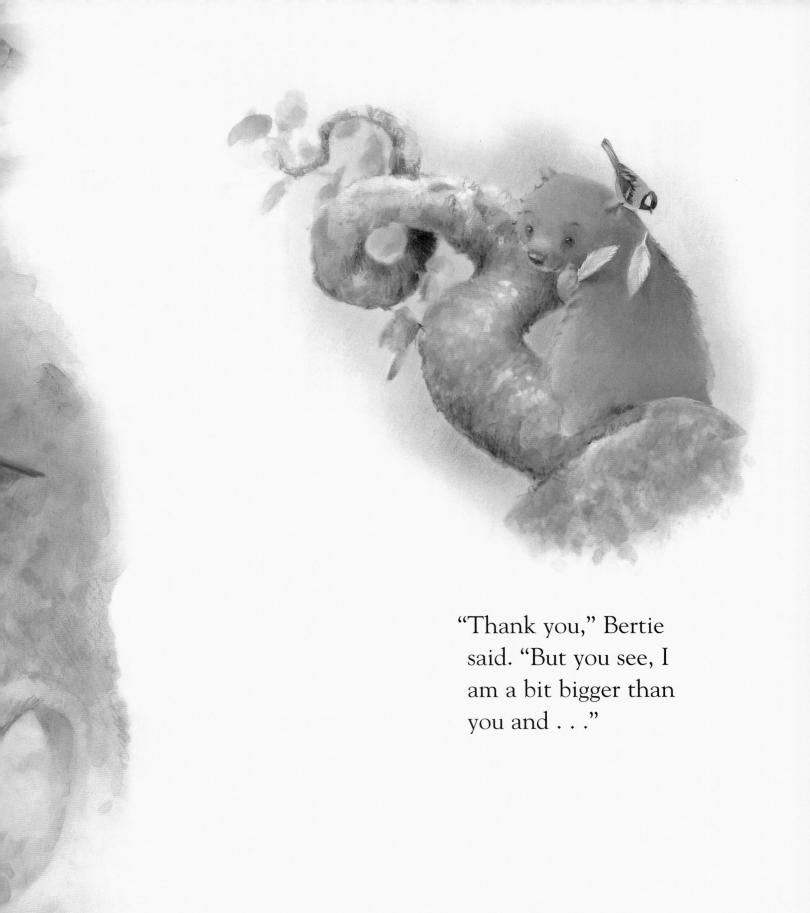

"Thank you," Bertie
said. "But you see, I
am a bit bigger than
you and . . ."

Just then Bertie saw a blanket in the tree!

"Wow!" said Bertie. "This must be a
pancake-blanket tree!"

He wrapped himself up and felt warm
and snuggly.

"If you're cold, you can always come here,"
he called to the birds.

Bertie loved the moonlight. But then clouds
moved in front of the moon and Bertie was a
little afraid.

Some glow-worms came to him with their
tiny lamps. But they were not quite right for
a little bear who was scared of the dark.

"That's very kind," Bertie said, "but . . ."

All of a sudden it was bright!
The light came from a lantern
dangling nearby.

"Ooh! This is a pancake-
blanket-lantern tree," said
Bertie. "Anyone who's scared
of the dark can join me!"

But there was silence all around.
The squirrels and birds had gone
to sleep, and the glow-worms
had put out their lamps.

Bertie saw the light of the Bear
House and wished he was there.
He wanted to tell Mummy Bear
and Baby Bear about the magic
pancake-blanket-lantern tree
and all the kind animals.

Bertie gathered the remaining
pancakes and the blanket and
the lantern and clambered
down the tree.

Quietly he opened the door
to the Bear House.

"Look what I've brought you and Baby Bear from my magic tree!" he said, as Mummy Bear gave him a big hug. "I never knew, but it's a pancake-blanket-lantern tree!"

"What's a pancake-blanket-
   lantern tree?" whispered Baby
Bear. Mummy Bear smiled.
   "I'll take you there tomorrow!"
said Bertie, and he fell fast
asleep as Mummy Bear tucked
him up in bed.